Copyright © 2001 De Vier Windstreken, an imprint of Nord-Süd Verlag AG, Gossau Zürich, Switzerland
First published in Holland under the title *Koen wil een wolk*.
English translation copyright © 2001 by North-South Books Inc.

All rights reserved. No part of this book may be reproduced or utilized in any form or by any means, electronic or mechanical, including photocopying, recording, or any information storage and retrieval system, without permission in writing from the publisher.

First published in the United States, Great Britain, Canada, Australia, and New Zealand in 2001 by North-South Books, an imprint of Nord-Süd Verlag AG, Gossau Zürich, Switzerland.
Distributed in the United States by North-South Books Inc., New York.
Library of Congress Cataloging-in-Publication Data is available.
A CIP catalogue record for this book is available from The British Library.
ISBN 0-7358-1525-9 (trade binding) 10 9 8 7 6 5 4 3 2 1
ISBN 0-7358-1526-7 (library binding) 10 9 8 7 6 5 4 3 2 1
Printed in Belgium
For more information about our books, and the authors and artists who create them, visit our web site: www.northsouth.com

Ken's Cloud

By Isabel M. Arqués
Illustrated by Angela Pelaez

North-South Books / New York / London

Ken was bored with all his toys.
He wanted something different.
A cloud would be nice, he thought.

So Ken climbed on top of the roof.

He saw a   white cloud overhead.
"Will you come and play with me?" he asked.

Ken took the white cloud back to his room.
He sat on his bed and watched the cloud rise
right up to the ceiling.

"Now I want it to rain," Ken told the cloud.
"Don't be silly," replied the cloud. "Don't you know
that only dark storm clouds can make rain?"

So Ken got out his brush and climbed up
to paint the cloud.

And sure enough, it started to rain.

It rained harder and harder.
Thunder roared and lightning flashed!

Ken wasn't afraid.
He grabbed a lightning bolt and pretended to fight.

Ken drew an eye patch on his cloud.
"Now you look just like a pirate," he said.

It kept on raining.
The water rose higher and higher.

Suddenly, a shark appeared,
ready to eat Ken's teddy bear!

Ken opened his bedroom door.
The water rushed out and so did the shark.

"Whew!" said Ken. "That was a close call!"

"Now I want it to snow," Ken told the cloud.
"Don't be silly," replied the cloud. "Don't you know
that only white clouds can make snow?"

So Ken got out his brush
and climbed back up to paint the cloud.

And sure enough, it started to snow.

It snowed harder and harder.
It was a real blizzard!

But before long, Ken began to shiver from the cold.

Ken drew a sweater on his cloud.
"Now you look nice and warm," he said.

Then Ken opened the window. "Good-bye, cloud.
Thanks for coming to play with me," he said.
Then he blew and blew as hard as he could,
and the cloud floated out of the window.

Ken was bored with all his toys.
He wanted something different.

The sun would be nice, he thought.